RICHARD WEIHE

Pe

HE GERMAN

Meer der
Tusche

AUTHOR

Richard Weihe studied drama and philosophy in Zurich and Oxford. His poetic biographies of influential artists have earned him a wide readership. *Sea of Ink*, published in Switzerland in 2005, won the Prix des Auditeurs de la Radio Suisse Romande. In 2010 he published *Ocean of Milk* based on the life of the Indian-Hungarian painter Amrita Sher-Gil.

TRANSLATOR

Jamie Bulloch has worked as a professional translator from German since 2001. His works include books by Paulus Hochgatterer and Alissa Walser. Jamie has also translated *Portrait of the Mother as a Young Woman* by FC Delius (Title No 3) and *The Mussel Feast* by Brigit Vanderbeke (Title No 10) for Peirene.

MEIKE ZIERVOGEL
PEIRENE PRESS

Fact and fiction arrive at a perfect union in this exquisite novella. A beautiful story about the quiet, determined pursuit of inspiration, this is a charming and uplifting book. After reading it, I looked at the world a little differently.

First published in Great Britain in 2012 by
Peirene Press Ltd
17 Cheverton Road
London N19 3BB
www.peirenepress.com

First published under the original title *Meer der Tusche*
by Nagel & Kimche, 2003
© Richard Weihe, 2003
Reprinted 2014

This translation © Jamie Bulloch, 2012

This work has been published with the financial assistance of the
Swiss Arts Council Pro Helvetia.

swiss arts council

prohelvetia

ISBN 978-0-9562840-8-2

Designed by Sacha Davison Lunt
Typeset by Tetragon
Photographic image: Pixmann / Imagezoo / Getty Images
Printed and bound by T J International, Padstow, Cornwall
Supported by:

LOTTERY FUNDED

Peirene

RICHARD WEIHE

TRANSLATED FROM THE GERMAN BY JAMIE BULLOCH

Sea
of Ink

1 Having ridden through the night, the messengers reached the northern frontier at midday on the 26th of April and handed over a letter to the commanding general, Wu Sangui. It stated that the rebel leader, Li Zicheng, had invaded Peking the previous day and occupied the capital. Facing impending disaster, the emperor had hanged himself. The future of the dynasty was dangling in the air.

The general had been given the task of securing the frontier against the Manchu people, the name the united Jurchen tribes of Manchuria had given themselves. The city of Shenyang they had renamed Mukden. From their new capital they gradually extended their power westwards into the borderland with China and as far as the Great Wall.

Under severe pressure General Wu resorted to desperate measures: he opened the border and asked the powerful Manchus for help in a campaign against the rebel Li. The neighbours agreed at once to stand side by side with their foe. Joining forces, the armies that had only recently been enemies succeeded in driving Li from the capital. It was the 2nd of June.

General Wu's troops went in pursuit of the insurgents as they withdrew to the west. On the 6th of June the Manchus took Peking for themselves without encountering any resistance. Their conquest of China had begun. It was early summer, 1644. The Manchus brought the three-hundred-year reign of the Ming dynasty to an end and proclaimed the dawn of a new era.

The south of the vast empire had not yet been taken, however.

2 With his countless wives and concubines, the founder of the Ming dynasty had thirty-two children, twenty-six of which were sons. His seventeenth son was born in 1378. The boy was given the title of the first Prince of Ning and he established the Ning line of the imperial house. The emperor invested him with the province of Jiangxi, which lay to the south of the Yangtze river. Its capital was Nanchang, and for centuries Nanchang remained the seat of the Ning line. The prince with twenty-five brothers had many children himself. One of his innumerable descendants, Zhu Da, was born in 1626, in the eleventh generation of the Yiyang branch of the Ning line.

This story is about Zhu Da, the Prince of Yiyang, distant descendant of the Prince of Ning, the seventeenth son of the founder of the Ming dynasty.

As a prince, Zhu Da enjoyed a sheltered childhood in the palace, surrounded by splendour and wealth. At the age of eight he started writing poetry. Early on he also displayed a special gift for seal-cutting. He was spoilt and admired because of his talents. These were blissful years full of promise for the future.

3 Zhu's father worked as a painter and calligrapher. His father, too, had been a much-revered painter and scholar.

Zhu's grandfather had made him a scroll painting of a dragon for his bedroom. The young Zhu thought this dragon was the largest creature that had ever existed. Its sinuous body writhed in rhythmic loops and looked so lifelike that each morning Zhu was glad to see his dragon had not changed position in the picture.

In his dreams the fire-spitting monster broke free from the paper and little Zhu had to leap into the water to save himself. He would dive under and the flames would turn to steam as they hissed on the surface. Looking up through the water, he could see the dragon's green shimmering eyes and flared nostrils in a cloud of steam. Even in the light of the morning, the dragon looked as if it might fly away at any moment or escape by setting fire to the paper surrounding it. The monster's scaly skin drifted between green and turquoise depending on how the light fell.

And yet his grandfather had not used any colours, only black ink on brownish paper.

On one of his earliest birthdays his father painted him a huge lotus flower. Zhu had never seen one of these flowers before, nor did he know its name.

His father placed a large piece of rice paper on the ground and picked up a brush with compact bristles. He dipped it in ink and wiped off the excess on a stone shaped like a peach. Then, with one long, rich stroke of his brush, he painted a gentle curve from the bottom to the top of the paper. Beneath his hand the upper end of the line unfurled into a flower.

At the base of the flower stem his father painted a surface of glistening grey across the entire width of the paper, occasionally allowing the brush to create darker patches. When the ink was dry he hung the painted paper on the wall.

Now Zhu noticed the lotus flower's slender stem shooting up from dirty, muddy water and opening its bloom in the clear spring air.

Some leaves were floating on the water and Zhu thought he could feel a gentle breeze sweeping across the surface, faintly bending the stem and wafting the perfume of the flower into his nose.

His father sat there calmly, frowning at the paper, and said nothing. Perhaps at that very moment he would have liked to talk about the flower that was hanging on the wall to his son, who was gazing at it wide-eyed and with lips pressed shut.

But his father remained silent. Zhu had never heard his father speak. And yet he felt as if he knew his voice.

They sat there beside each other, looking at the picture. All of a sudden Zhu thought he could hear a rattling from his father's throat and he grabbed his arm. But his father had said nothing; he merely turned his head, fixed the boy with his old, watery eyes, and the line between his lips turned up a whisker at the ends.

'You just gurgled then, Father,' Zhu said. 'Like a fish underwater.'

He fixed his gaze on the lotus flower once more.

The fish remained silent.

'I expect you've told me everything already.'

4 On one occasion his father made him step barefoot into a bowl full of ink and then walk along the length of a roll of paper. To begin with, Zhu's footprints were wet and black; with each step they became lighter until they were barely visible any more. Then he hopped from the paper back onto the wooden floor.

His father took a brush and wrote at the top of the scroll: *A small segment of the long path of my son Zhu Da.* And further down: *A path comes into existence by being walked on.*

The palace had its own workshop for manufacturing brushes and ink. Zhu liked to watch the master and his assistants at work. The open stoves made the workshop dingy and dusty. The fire, Zhu thought, so that's where he gets his colourful dragon, and the lotus flower too.

One day, after Zhu pleaded with him insistently, the master explained how ink is made.

'To make ink we need two ingredients,' he said, 'soot and glue. The soot provides the colour, the glue binds it. We mix them together, working them into a kneadable paste in mortars. We then press the paste into carved wooden moulds and let it dry until it's completely hard.'

'What's soot?' Zhu wanted to know.

'In the forest we collect resinous branches from old pine trees. We burn them in the stove. What remains afterwards is a fine black powder. This powder is the soot.'

'And how do you make the glue?'

'To make glue we order stags' antlers from Dai province. We cut the horns into finger-length pieces and place these in the river. They stay in the water for twelve days and twelve nights until they're washed through and clean. Then we put the pieces in a large pan. If you cook them for long enough they turn into a thick sludge. If you cook them for even longer they eventually turn into glue. And the glue and soot need to be pounded thirty thousand times in the iron mortar to mix them properly.'

The master encouraged him to peer into the huge pan where a soup with chunks of stags' antlers was boiling away, but Zhu held his nose and turned aside fast.

'That stinks!'

'I agree, the smell is somewhat unpleasant. It always troubled your father, too. So he developed his own recipe.'

The master took a small bottle from the shelf.

'Here, take a sniff, Prince.'

A pleasant, spicy aroma wafted into Zhu's nose.

'That's a mixture of cloves, camphor and musk. We use it as a perfume. It has a stronger aroma than the glue.'

Now the master held a second phial under his nose. Zhu was instantly taken by the fruity, heady smell.

'An infusion of bark from the pomegranate tree,' the master said. 'Your father always adds this secret preparation. That's why his ink is called "The envoy of the pomegranate tree".'

The master raised his forefinger and looked Zhu sternly in the eye.

'But you didn't hear a word from me, my prince.'

5 At the age of thirteen, Zhu Da enrolled in Nan-chang as a student for entry into the civil service.

A glittering future lay before him: the life of a cultivated art-lover and man of letters, dividing his time between the study of beauty, managing provincial affairs and pleasure.

A few years later his family chose a girl from a good family as a suitable wife for the prince. In the very first year of their marriage she gave birth to a child.

This was also the year when the Ming dynasty came to an end and the Qing dynasty began.

First, the capital fell into the hands of the Manchus. But after the conquest of Peking the majority of the country remained under Chinese rule. From the capital the Manchus embarked on their systematic conquest of the entire empire. It did not take them long to win over Chinese collaborators for their campaign.

Nanking had long been regarded as a second capital city in the south. There the Ming princes were able to maintain their rule after the fall of Peking. But a struggle broke out over the succession. From among the many rivals a clique of influential officials finally named the Prince of Fu as emperor.

The Prince of Fu preferred the easy life. His father had tracked down and killed followers of the rebel Li. The prince now sent four armies northwards to the banks of the Yangtze as protection. But the four generals fought among themselves for supremacy. Instead of forming a united front against the Manchu onslaught, the soldiers marauded and plundered their way through the villages. Only one of the generals, Shi Kefa, showed the necessary resolve in the fight against the advancing enemy, until a faction of adversaries from Nanchang toppled him from power.

Zhu's home city of Nanchang lay to the south-west of Nanking, in the province of Jiangxi. There the prince lived with his wife and young son in the palace.

Dark clouds were gathering in the sky, but no storm had yet brushed the earth.

6 The Manchus retained their organization of the Eight Banners and began stationing garrisons of banner soldiers in key places. They adopted the existing Chinese administrative system without any major changes and did not touch the landowners' estates. They did not break their rice bowls, as the saying goes, for the Manchus were full of admiration for Chinese culture. And so it happened that scholars moved to the capital in droves to offer their services in administrative posts.

The government in Nanking tried negotiating with the Manchus. They sent an embassy to Peking to suggest that the Manchus limit their conquests to the area north of the Great Wall. But the envoys returned with the counter-suggestion that Nanking, too, should recognize the sovereignty of the new rulers. On that condition Nanking could remain as the seat of a vassal state in southern China.

Secretly, neither side was seriously interested in negotiations or any sort of compromise. While the envoys were still on their journey back to Nanking, the Manchus were preparing their army for the conquest of the south.

When they attacked the city of Yangzhou on the northern bank of the Yangtze, they encountered their first meaningful resistance. General Shi Kefa defended the city heroically against the offensive by superior forces. He held Yangzhou for eight days; on the ninth, the Manchus broke through the gates.

When they saw the soldiers flood in, the men cowered on the ground. Nobody dared take flight. They lowered their heads, bared their necks and waited for the swish of the sword. The young women tried to buy their lives with their bodies and offered themselves up to the soldiers. Some hid in rubbish heaps, smeared themselves with muck and sought to disguise themselves. But the soldiers prodded the refuse with spears until the last of them crawled out like startled rats.

The general was taken prisoner. In his situation many would have gone over to the Manchus. But he refused and remained loyal to his former masters.

Shi Kefa was executed in the most grisly way imaginable.

The Chinese general Hong Chengchou was one of those who sided with the enemy. After the fall of Yangzhou he led the Qing armies further south. In the summer of 1645 they stood at the gates of Nanking. The Prince of Fu's government collapsed under the pressure of this threat. One of his own generals handed the prince over to the Qing forces. They dragged him back to Peking and his fate was sealed. A few months later he was dead.

Some Ming princes were still trying to prolong the rule of their dynasty. Their attempts proved futile, however. The Prince of Lu set himself up as regent in Zhejiang province. But without resources and supplies he was unable to hold out for long.

Another, the Prince of Tang, was named emperor in August 1645. His closest ally was a former pirate, Zheng Zhilong, who had since blossomed into a wealthy businessman and official. As a military leader, however, Zheng was no match for the might of the Manchus.

When he finally surrendered, the conquerors were able to cross the mountain passes he had been guarding to Zhejiang and Fujian. Now the Manchus could continue their expansion into new prefectures and provinces unopposed.

The prince escaped to Hunan. Once there he found himself confronted by the last scattered troops of the rebel leader Li. His attempts to put together a powerful army failed. The prince fell into the hands of the Manchus and was executed on the spot.

His younger brother managed to flee to Canton, where he lasted another two months, a shadow of the former ruling power. When the Qing troops, led by a turncoat Chinese general, finally invaded Canton, the shadow vanished too. The sun of the Ming dynasty was extinguished.

7 When power changed hands Zhu's father died. The Prince of Yiyang had just turned nineteen. At the court he had earned a reputation as a speaker with a sparkling wit; in debate he was indefatigable.

Now he stared tight-lipped at his dead father and said nothing. The same image reappeared in his mind's eye: the long stem of a lotus flower snapping in the wind and falling into the dirty water of a pond where the white bloom gradually sank.

He did not say anything the following day, either, when his wife addressed him several times. He behaved like this on the third and fourth days, too.

These days became weeks. Zhu had forgotten how to speak.

One day he got up and painted a large symbol on his door: *ya* – dumb.

The news of the master's death spread amongst calligraphers and many came to express their condolences to Zhu. He received them with animated gestures and meaningful looks, but did not exchange a single word with any of them. In conversation he made use of his hands and his entire body. If he was in agreement with somebody he would nod; if not, he shook his head vigorously.

Or he just stared into the distance.

In the evenings he drank liquor with old friends of his father's. They told him of the turmoil in the country and the atrocities they had seen. Suddenly Zhu got up and started laughing and crying in turn. Later he sang songs.

At least I'm not dead, he thought. But what use is not being dead? If I were a fish I'd simply dive down into the depths. At the moment I'm like a fish out of water.

8 Nothing changed over the following months and years. He began to fast, physically and spiritually. It was as if he had been turned to stone. People would find him half naked, without a shirt, sitting on the floor with his legs apart, utterly still.

When the Manchus invaded Jiangxi province and attacked the city of Nanchang, they occupied the palace. Zhu Da hurriedly separated from his wife and young son and fled to the Fengxin mountains, a few days' ride to the north-west of the city. There he entered a monastery.

He shaved his head and, as a monk, took the name Chuanqi. In the peace and solitude of the monastery he buried himself in the study of Buddhist teaching.

As the last of the Mings, the Prince of Gui endeavoured to maintain rule in the south. He lived in Guandong, the province to the south of Jiangxi, but soon afterwards, in 1647, he was forced to flee to Guangxi province to the west. Following the twists and turns of the war, he spent the next dozen years drifting around south-west China, in the provinces of Sichuan and Guizhou as well. His warriors attacked wherever they could, without ever winning any ground. Over time they became worn down and once again divisions appeared within the Chinese ranks.

The prince himself was pursued by the Qing armies under the leadership of General Wu. He finally found refuge in Burma, although there they regarded him as a foe rather than a guest and he was held prisoner for several years. Wu maintained pressure on the Burmese until they finally handed over the prince and his family. The general led them to the east, into the remote province of Yunnan, where the Prince of Gui and his son were strangled with a bowstring.

Thus were the forces of the southern Mings wiped out. The prince's last loyal and devoted general died of grief when he heard of his master's downfall. Only bitterness and enmity remained.

Jesuits, who had come from distant Europe, worked at the court of the last Ming emperor. Under their influence the mother of the emperor, his wife and his son had converted to Christianity. In 1650 the Polish Jesuit Michał Boym left for Rome with a letter from the emperor addressed to the superior general of the Jesuits and the pope, begging for assistance to save the Ming dynasty.

After a two-year journey, Boym reached Venice. The pope's reply took three years and the envoy did not return to China until 1659. By now, all offers of assistance were too late. Nothing remained of the court and Michał Boym died that same year without having handed over the papal message.

As soon as Qing rule had been consolidated, the Jesuits returned to the court in Peking.

9 While the Qings severed the last few veins of the old dynasty, letting the blood seep away, in the monastery Chuanqi was studying the teachings of peace and quiet, Chuanqi the monk who had once been a prince called Zhu Da.

The old empire was destroyed, but the mountains of Fengxin were still the same. The trees and rivers had not changed, and the cawing of the crows sounded no different from before.

In 1653 Chuanqi was admitted to the small circle of pupils of Abbot Hongmin. Four years later he completed his master's examination. Now he was qualified to pass on the tenets of Buddhist wisdom to the younger scholars.

His former life as a prince seemed ever more unreal, as if it had been a lengthy preparation for the path he had now chosen.

'Teach yourself how not to get involved,' the abbot said. 'Do not act; rather acquaint yourself with the feeling of wanting to act, but not doing so. Only act when what you are able to do corresponds with what you wish to do.'

The abbot smiled and added, 'We were all princes once.'

Sometimes Chuanqi would stroll down into town, driven by curiosity to see what had changed. He wandered through the streets, gesticulating wildly and creating quite a sensation with his sobbing fits and outbursts of screaming. In the local taverns he drank wine until he fell down senseless.

People thought he was a madman.

Nobody knew, or even suspected, that inside Chuanqi the monk was the Prince of Yiyang from the last generation of the Ming dynasty.

The silence in the temple comforted him. He learnt to forget and he felt a powerful sense of calm permeate his whole being.

The pavilion afforded an expansive view across the plain to a distant chain of hills. One day – it was winter and had been snowing – he stood with the master by the balustrade on the terrace, enjoying the fantastic view.

'Chuanqi,' the abbot said, 'you see the faintly curved line of the distant horizon in the snow? Practise absorbing this line inside you. Become one with things and flow away with them. This is the basic rule for preserving life.'

In spring, when the snow had melted, Chuanqi appeared before the master and said, 'That line you talked about: I've absorbed it.'

Without moving, Abbot Hongmin gave him a long stare. Then he said, 'Chuanqi, it is now time to discard your novice's name. Today I will give you a new one. From now on you will be called Xuege – snow aside. You are now a master of the inner world and ready for the teachings of the outer world.'

10 Abbot Hongmin knew of Xuege's desire to become a painter, but until then he had strictly forbidden him to touch a paintbrush. On that day in spring 1658, in the fourteenth year of the Qing dynasty, he believed the moment had come to begin the painting lessons.

The master gave Xuege a brush which was as long as his legs and as thick as a young tree trunk. He instructed his pupil to stretch out his arms and hold the brush by its loop so that the tips of the bristles just touched the floor.

In the tea room the master had made a large square with rolls of rice paper. The abbot pointed to a wooden tub in the corner and said, 'Dip the brush into the bucket and wipe off the ink a few times on the rim. Then go back to your place without delay.'

When the brush was saturated with black ink it was considerably heavier. Xuege had trouble lifting it high enough to wipe it on the edge of the tub. He returned to his place, held the brush with outstretched arms as the master had instructed and watched a black dot appear on the paper, which began expanding rapidly as the ink flowed out.

The master stood behind him, breathing words into Xuege's ear: 'Pace out a circle, painting it as you move. Keep going in a circle until the trace of your brush has faded.'

His muscles tensed, Xuege held the brush vertically over the sheet so that the tips of the bristles were just touching the paper, and moved forwards, step by step. After the first circle Hongmin noticed that Xuege's lips were pressed tightly shut.

'You should paint, not stop breathing.'

In fact Xuege had great difficulty concentrating on the brush tip and the imaginary midpoint of his circle at the same time. He could not stop and rest because he would waste ink; moreover it was almost harder to hold the brush while standing still.

Xuege went on and the shining black bristles left behind a thin trace on the paper. After another circle his teacher said, 'You went in a circle but you did not draw one. Do not make any detours. Go on, improve the circle.'

The abbot said no more as Xuege completed his third, fourth and fifth circles. Then he forgot to count. Each step became a torture. He was just blindly following his own track.

The line became ever fatter, for the brush sank lower and lower with Xuege's vanishing strength. His arms trembled and the brush transferred even the slightest movement onto the paper.

The abbot now sounded dictatorial: 'Your line is starting to shudder, Xuege. Let it go on for as long as there is still ink left. Stand up straight. Listen to what I tell you!'

After another half-turn Xuege's back started giving way. But all of a sudden he felt the short, sharp stroke of a bamboo cane in his side. He completed the circle. Was it the ninth? Or the tenth? His master's gaze burnt into his back, but he knew that he would not be able to manage yet another circle.

Then he collapsed on top of the brush. His body fell onto the cluster of bristles, squashing them so that the last remaining ink flowed out and made large dark stains on the paper as well as on his white robe. He looked like a dying man lying in his own blood.

When Xuege glanced up, his face contorted with pain, expecting a second, possibly harder stroke of the bamboo cane, he saw his master's severe expression.

'If you ever wish to become a Master of the Great Ink you must learn to hold the brush firmly. Let it go only when no ink is left. Never before.'

11

For many months he drew large circles with the heavy brush.

One day the master unexpectedly ordered Xuege to rebuild a derelict monastery complex in a remote spot in the Fengxin mountains.

Xuege devoted himself to this task with all his energy. The renovation of the temple took six years.

The new monastery was called Green Cloud.

From then on he lived in the solitude of the mountains, immersing himself ever deeper in the teachings of the Tao. His responsibilities as the leader of a community of monks prevented him from leaving the Green Cloud for lengthy periods of time, but not from receiving friends and acquaintances as guests.

One evening he went into the pine forest alone. The mountain peaks were glowing in the evening light. It appeared as if a giant had carved them with a huge knife. The flat rocks looked so clean, as if they had been washed. The stream snaked its way upwards, ending in a mere silver thread.

When Xuege spotted a swathe of white flowers along the riverbank he took off his shoes, walked over, bent down and greeted them as if they were children. He had a sudden, burning desire to see all the flowers of Jiangxi in one evening. He ran barefoot across the springy floor of the pine forest; he was dancing with the earth. The light and the pines and the stream and the flowers were there for him alone, and in his happiness Xuege forgot his exhaustion and sorrow, and his heart became as light as a feather.

If you are guided by human feelings you will easily

lose your way, a wise saying went, but if you are guided by nature you will rarely go wrong.

Now he had understood.

He finally sat down. The place was so quiet and remote; no monk ever found his way here. He thought: Even if I sat here for three hundred years the mountains would not fall.

A formation of wild geese passed over him like an arrow of feathers seeking to strike desire itself. The stone he was sitting on and the entire ground under him seemed to melt away.

I'd like to live here for the rest of my life, he told himself, until I die on this mountain.

Then he recalled his life as Zhu Da, as a young prince, and he recalled his wife's black hair and his son's first smile.

But these images were not memories, rather the dream of a life never lived.

12 The following day he woke with a terrible heaviness in his heart. Somebody seemed to be calling him; he thought he could hear a distant voice but could not understand it. Gripped by an inner urge, he went to his desk, where every day for years he had completed the drawing exercises the master had set him.

He poured some water into the hollow of the rubbing stone, took the hard block of ink and rubbed it. Then he selected one of his finer brushes and dipped it in.

He had laid a square piece of yellowy-white paper on the desk, which was around four hand's widths in size. At the lower edge and slightly to the left, he set down the paintbrush, drawing it upwards in a gentle curve, half a finger's width, which started to the left then changed direction halfway up the paper. A second later he applied a little more pressure to the brush and veered it back to the left. He let this thickened line run to a black point that almost touched the edge of the paper and, without lifting the paintbrush, cocked his wrist, whereupon the tips of the bristles pirouetted; and now the brush glided back down the line in the opposite direction, and beyond onto the blank paper; then with another turn of the wrist he brought his hand down towards himself, lifting the brush from the paper in a slow but fluid movement so that the bottom of his line tapered as evenly as the top had.

And without adding more ink to the brush, he immediately covered the bottom third of the paper with wave-like shapes stacking up to the right, either with a flick of his wrist or by pressing down his hand to leave black

Lotus flower

streaks which came out darker or lighter depending on the pressure. Just before the paintbrush ran out of ink he took it to the upper right-hand corner of the paper and, holding it vertically, signed the picture with the name Geshan – single mountain.

Then he put his brush aside. To finish, he printed his seal in red ink beneath the signature.

He went out onto the terrace, gripped the balustrade and closed his eyes.

Geshan had painted his first picture.

After a while he returned to his desk and looked at the lotus flower which had appeared on the paper. Its black-painted bloom looked white and lit up his signature in the corner.

Why did he think he could recognize himself in the line of the flower stem and the outlines of the petal?

When he placed his right hand on the white, unpainted part of the paper he noticed that the stem and the lower part of the flower traced the outline of his thumb and wrist almost exactly. With ink he had painted a flower, and with the area he had left blank he had depicted part of his hand.

The flower grew out of the swamp and slime into the air above, there to unfurl its beauty in clear, sharp outlines.

13 Geshan alias Xuege alias Chuanqi alias Zhu Da brought the lotus flower painting to Master Hongmin for appraisal. He said, 'I can see that you have grasped much already. You have understood the sense of form and three-dimensional shape; your brush is able to express the curve of the stem and the surface of the petals; it can portray light and colours. You have learnt to see blackness not as an obstacle, but as a source. Here the black depicts a shining white; there, a muted brown or a transparent greenish-blue. You have, moreover, made good progress in understanding the essence of things. Your brush suggests some of the floweriness of the flower and the wateriness of the water. That is much already. But there are still lessons you need to learn to master the black ink.'

'Which ones?'

'It is not my place to tell you that. You must happen upon it for yourself. But you will know when the right moment has come. That I do not doubt.'

'Master, give me at least a clue as to how I can improve myself.'

'You will find all the answers inside yourself. Are you nothing more than a combination of various types and forms of surface? Why should your picture be created only from stiff outer layers that lack all sensibility?'

Geshan gave him an enquiring look. After a while the master added, 'When you paint you do not speak. But when you have painted, your brush should have said everything. When it has learnt how to speak you will be a Master of the Great Ink.'

14 Geshan had been running the Monastery of the Green Cloud for several years and his reputation as a master of the Tao had spread throughout the entire province. One day the artist Huang Anping paid him a visit to paint his portrait. Geshan agreed on the condition that he could dress up for it.

While Huang prepared to paint and rubbed the ink, Geshan went down to the river. He asked a fisherman to lend him his straw hat and shoes. In the monastery he borrowed a white robe from one of the monks.

He stood before the painter with his hands in front of his chest so that the wide sleeves hung down heavily in long folds. His feet were in black sandals and he gazed out sceptically from beneath the broad brim of the fisherman's hat which covered his head like a huge lotus flower.

The year was 1674.

The Manchus had brought the entire country under their dominion. As they venerated Chinese culture, they tried to win over artists and scholars. The final scattered members of the old dynasty were accorded special recognition by the Manchus.

Huang Anping told all of this to Geshan as they sat together drinking that evening. They decided to disclose the identity of the fisherman in the picture and so, next to his portrait of Geshan, Huang Anping wrote: *Scion of the imperial line of the Ming dynasty*.

But how had Huang managed to convey the imperial destiny in the facial features of the fisherman? To begin with, the small figure of Geshan stood utterly lost against the empty white background. But Geshan invited special visitors to the Monastery of the Green Cloud to leave behind their seal or a verse on his portrait. His friends Rao Yupu, Peng Wenliang and Cai Shou covered the blank space with their calligraphy, expressing their esteem for the man in the fisherman's hat. Gradually the background was filled with seals, sayings and testimonies of friendship until they bordered the figure.

15 Geshan discussed with the master the relationship between the tall mountain and the small piece of paper, between the hardness of the rock and the softness of the paintbrush.

'How is it possible to express magnitude through smallness, hardness through softness and light through darkness? How can one thing be expressed by another which it is not?'

'You need to overcome the contradictions in your mind,' the master began. 'Learn to combine them as you do ink and brush. A thing is a thing in relationship to itself, but also in relationship to other things. It is this as well as that. Even if we comprehend the thing only from the perspective of the this, it is nonetheless determined by both this *and* that.'

The master paused for a moment.

'Do not, therefore, become enslaved by the perspective of absolute opposites. This is also that, and that is also this,' he reiterated. 'At the point they cease to be in opposition you find the axis of the Path. The Path becomes obscured if you walk down it only one way.'

'Your words themselves are obscure, Master,' Geshan said. 'How does what you say influence the handling of the brush?'

'For me as a painter the value of the mountain is not in its size, but in the possibility of mastering it with the paintbrush. When you look at a mountain you are seeing a piece of nature. But when you paint a mountain it becomes a mountain. You do not paint its size, you imply it. The importance of the brush lies not in the extent of its bristles, but in the traces it leaves behind.

The importance of the ink lies not in the ink, but in the power of expression and mutability of its flow. The importance of the mountain stream lies not in itself, but in its movement; the importance of the mountain lies in its silence.'

Then he continued: 'Your hand is your guiding spirit. You have everything in your hand. The line that unites is contained in all things.'

And he added: 'When you dip your paintbrush into the ink, you are dipping it into your soul. And when you guide the paintbrush, it is your spirit guiding it. Without depth and saturation your ink lacks soul; without guidance and liveliness your brush lacks spirit. The one thing receives from the other. The stroke receives from the ink, the ink receives from the brush, the brush receives from the wrist and the wrist receives from your guiding spirit. That means mastering the power of both ink and brush.'

16 One day the master summoned him and said, 'It is important that you paint only with the best ink and the best brushes.'

'How will I recognize the best ink?'

'It should breathe in the light like the feathers of a raven and shine like the pupils in a child's eyes.'

The master invited Geshan to sit down in the middle of the room with his back to the light and instructed him not to move.

'I will teach you how to spot the difference between everyday ink and superlative ink.'

The abbot disappeared behind a screen. After a while he came back with a piece of paper. Geshan read out loud the sentence the master had just written: *'It is not the man who wears the ink down, but the ink that wears the man down.'*

'Do not think about these words now,' the master said. 'Look only at the blackness of the symbols and remember the features of this blackness.'

The master let him ponder this for a while, then vanished behind the screen with the paper. Soon afterwards he reappeared with a second piece of paper, on which he had written the same sentence. Now he challenged Geshan to say whether the second sentence had been written with the same ink as the first.

Geshan held the paper up to the light, paying particular attention to the characters for 'man' and 'ink'. He was unable to detect any obvious differences in the quality of the ink.

'Which writing is blacker – the first or the second?' the master asked.

'I don't see a difference,' Geshan admitted.

The master threw his hands up in the air and exclaimed, 'One must be an expert to recognize unusual things! To be a painter it is not sufficient to be able to distinguish pebbles from jade and fish eyes from pearls. As a painter you must be able to distinguish black from black; they are very different things! People look at an ink's blackness only because we require ink to be black, and ink that is not black is surely worthless. That is true. However, if the ink is merely black but not shining, then it appears dull and colourless, and so it is useless. It needs to be both black and shining, and this lustre must shimmer like the surface of the water when the light changes – clear, pure water through which you can see the ground. Then the ink is sublime!'

Without waiting for an answer, the master went behind the screen once more and presented his pupil with a third piece of paper.

'The blackness of this ink has an almost metallic sheen; it shimmers like varnish,' Geshan thought as he held the characters close to his eyes. Then he said, 'That's a different ink!'

The master leapt up, hurried behind the screen, held the first two pieces of paper in front of Geshan and ripped them up under his nose.

'You identified it! As you rightly said, there is no difference between the first and second pieces of paper. Both of them were painted with the same everyday ink. Characters written in this ink arouse a feeling of displeasure and resistance in the viewer, for they are not really black and they lack any sheen. But for this piece of paper I used the ink of the ink-maker Pan Gu. It is unsurpassed and very difficult to come by. As you identified it, I shall reward you with two balls of his ink. They were given to me years ago by Privy Councillor Han Weisheng and to this day I have never dared use them. Keep them. You yourself will best know when you are ready to use them. Pan Gu's ink with the stamp of Han Weisheng is properly black. He mixed it with carp gall, which is what gives the ink its silky sheen, and the power of its colour comes from the addition of a little cinnabar and green walnut shells, the precise quantities of which are Pan Gu's secret.'

After a pause he went on: 'The man who spends his whole life painting with a single colour must not ignore such differences.'

17

Geshan wandered across the rocky heath near to the monastery and thought about the things the master had told him.

Once back in his room he sat at the desk by the window and stared at the mountain on the horizon.

He rubbed the ink he usually worked with, the ink which he had saved from his father's workshop. The balls from Pan Gu were in a safe place.

He covered the small piece of paper he had laid out with a few rapidly executed vertical and horizontal strokes. In the right half of the picture he interrupted a downwards sweep by lifting the brush and, from the centre of the paper, painted a broad line which he guided along a gentle incline to the right-hand edge of the paper, then made a straight brushstroke from the end of this down to the bottom with a single fluid movement of the hand.

With irregular strokes he drew two round shapes at the bottom of the paper and between these applied his brush a dozen times to form triangular patches of ink. Several times he covered the same small section of the paper with these softly contoured triangles to produce a many-layered area of ink in a variety of shades of black.

He enveloped the round shapes by dashing the tip of the brush rhythmically across the entire width of the paper to leave fine marks. Finally, in a gentle wave-like movement, he added a few longer, diagonal strokes above the round shapes, running from left to right. But at the very top, to one of the detached horizontal lines that stretched almost a third of the way across, he added a dense cluster of rough, spiky strokes; and directly beneath the horizontal line, set in the corner, he drew an elongated rectangle until his paintbrush had released its last drop of ink.

He dipped it in briefly a second time, just the tips of the bristles, to sign his picture with a new name. He wrote: 'Renwu' – human space.

He printed his seal in the corner.

The ink was soon dry. He attached the picture to the wall to view it from a distance.

Now he could see two stones on coarse grass, nestling up to a larger boulder. In their shelter grew a modest mountain flower with many leaves, watched over by the rough-edged rock. It gazed proudly and rebelliously through its eye slits and its hair spiked upwards like the spines of a hedgehog preparing to defend itself.

Renwu recognized himself not in the boulder, but in the tiny plant. The fortune to be oneself was sufficient for the plant to sit at the centre of the world.

Calamus

18 In the temple at the Monastery of the Green Cloud, Geshan, who now called himself Renwu, learnt of the death of his wife and son.

He had almost forgotten his time as Zhu Da, as a prince and husband and father.

Now the memories of the past stabbed him like knives.

From that day he let his hair grow again.

He went into town more frequently. He scanned the facial features of the women for a lost expression, a smile that no longer existed.

He recalled once more the moment when the court announced that they had found a suitable woman for him and that the marriage had been arranged.

'You will marry and have children, for whoever breaks the ancestral chain forsakes the very thing by which he became a descendant.'

Did he have to fear once more that he would remain without descendants?

He wanted to obey Confucian law and continue his line.

So now he entertained the idea of starting a family again.

19

He went to his pupils and told them he would be leaving the monastery.

After appointing his successor he removed his priestly robe and burnt it.

He tied together his picture album, packed away his collection of paintbrushes and ink and went down into the valley.

He looked back at the mountain and the Monastery of the Green Cloud. He had spent twenty years there, reconstructing the building and introducing his own strict rules. More than one hundred monks had been instructed by him.

The year was 1680 and now, over fifty years old, he wanted to reconnect with the past. He thought of the old saying: Falling leaves return to their roots.

But what was he now? Where was home to him? What was his name? He needed to find answers to everything.

He had placed all his pictures and painting things in a few sandalwood boxes which his pupils had given him as a leaving present. Inside he found pieces of paper on which each of the pupils had written some farewell words. They moved him greatly.

As he was crossing a river one evening he was set upon by highwaymen. Because the boxes were heavy, the highwaymen may have thought that they contained jade and gold. They stole the whole lot without opening them.

This incident troubled him for many weeks and during this time he kept his distance from other people, speaking to nobody.

He strove to recall his pupils' words from memory, to write down everything and thereby recover his lost treasure piece by piece. The only possessions that remained were a brush and Pan Gu's balls of ink, for he always carried these next to his body.

And not a single day passed when he did not paint or fill paper with calligraphy. Now, however, he merely signed his pictures with the character *lü*. Lü meant ass. *Bald ass* was a nickname for monks.

20 In the same year that he returned to Nanchang he married for a second time. She was a beautiful woman from a modest background to whom he did not disclose his true origins.

As a wedding present he gave her a fan which he had painted. On the fan was a large, round moon, beside it a branch with a single blossom and beneath were the words: *Words spoken by kindred souls have the fragrance of orchids.*

That same day he painted another picture in his album. Below it he wrote the lines: *Above Nanchang in the middle of autumn the moon stands alone. At midnight smoke rises from the censer in the form of a dragon. The dream vanishes in a dark cloud. The beautiful lady wears a long silk ribbon. The wind blows, but cannot catch it.*

He signed this picture with yet another new name which now he used alongside Lü: Poyun Qiaozhe – woodcutter of the evaporated clouds.

But he and his young bride did not find happiness together. He felt as if he were floating in a dark cloud, and what he could see through it seemed dismal and unreal. He remained restless.

He placed a card on his desk as a reminder and a warning. On it were the words: *Life and death matter.*

21

Acquaintances old and new tried to win him for their artistic circles. They organized poetry and music evenings in the hope that he would come.

Such events had become especially popular with the new ruling magistrates. And so one day Poyun Qiaozhe was invited by the venerable magistrate Hu Yitang to a poetry banquet, an invitation which would have required great diplomatic skill to decline. So he went along.

The host had hung every wall with empty sheets of paper. When all had assembled and plenty of wine had been passed round, he had one of his guests blindfolded: a young painter. The painter was taken from wall to wall and challenged to paint characters – made-up ones, but different each time. And each time the guests had to invent a name for the shape created by his brushstrokes. They came up with ideas such as *lotus leaf*, *death head*, *raindrop* and *broken jade clasp*. Or more fancy ones such as *dragon's head*, *silk thread*, *bundles of kindling*, *contorted cloud* and *untied rope*.

When a name had been agreed, it was written beneath the character. At night, in the darkness, the names were called out once more. Now the guests had to describe from memory the character associated with a particular name.

Lü, or Poyun Qiaozhe, as Zhu Da now called himself, tried to recreate the painter's brushstrokes with words as he fashioned the shape they had entitled *folded medal ribbon*. When the servant with the oil lamp then lit up the relevant character on the wall, everyone thought that Poyun had actually used his words as a brush, so precisely had the woodcutter of the evaporated clouds described the medal ribbon.

22 Poyun Qiaozhe was visited by one of his former pupils. The latter told him that old Abbot Hongmin was terminally ill and had called for him. They set off for the mountains together and found the master on his deathbed, in a temple outside the monastery complex.

'All I live on now is ginseng and other medicinal plants, but these do not help; it is too late. My body is a barren tree which waits for the crows of winter and will not see another summer. I am delighted that you have come. You are seeing me for the last time in this life.'

The old man pointed to a box by the wall.

'I am bequeathing you my paintbrushes. They must stay in motion. I know that you will use them wisely. You will not let them lie idle; you will capture on paper the mountains and lakes that you come across and you will not waste your time.'

It was spring and the door to the veranda had been pushed open, offering a view of the landscape bathed in a soft light.

'When you have my brushes in your hand, then remember my words,' the master said. 'The water that flows between the mountains and the sea will teach you all that you need to know to understand the world. It has the rare quality of being able to benefit all beings without dispute. Knowing the functions of the mountain without knowing the functions of the water is like the man who sinks into the sea without knowing its beaches or who stands on the beach without knowing the immense spaces which fill the sea.'

The master paused. Finally he said, 'Ink is water rendered visible, nothing more. The brush divides what is fluid from everything superfluous.'

23 When the dynasties changed in 1644, the Shun-zhi emperor, then a boy, was set on the Dragon Throne. He favoured Chinese officials and placed particular trust in the advice of the eunuchs. His defeat of the rebellion led by General Wu was an important step towards consolidating Manchu rule. When he died in 1661, still a young man, he was succeeded by his eight-year-old son, Kangxi.

Kangxi was greatly interested in classical Chinese culture and supported everything which helped to preserve tradition. Wherever possible he sought to cooperate with the native upper class and benefit from their knowledge.

After the master's death, Poyun avoided all occasions that he suspected had been organized by the new administration. One day, however, he received a request from the highest office of imperial government to take part, alongside the noble men of letters of the old regime, in a specially arranged examination officially designated as an 'Investigation into Great Scholarship'. The new rulers wished to write the history of their empire and for this they needed experts on previous eras.

Poyun was unable to dodge this summons. And so he sat the examination with a large number of hand-picked scholars.

Months later, when the results were assessed, he received an official invitation to place his knowledge as a historian of the Ming period at the disposal of the new rulers. The magistrate Hu Yitang invited him to spend a year in his residence, where, free of all worries, he would be able to devote himself to his art, on the condition that he collaborated in the great history project.

Poyun understood at once that this was not an invitation, but a veiled command which he must obey.

But he refused to serve the authorities. Instead he threw himself on the ground, yelling and howling; or he roamed through the town laughing, and talked to the swallows. He sat down right in the middle of the town square. Now he was drumming on his belly and singing rude songs; now he was dashing in a fury through the market stalls, hurling vegetables into the air.

The official responsible reported to the commission that Poyun had gone mad and so could not be recommended for working on the history of the former dynasty.

'He's mad? So why do the creations of his paintbrush have such immediacy and power?' the official was asked. 'And for what reason did the commission put him into the highest category of scholarship, the *Sea of Ink*?'

'What can I say?' the official replied. 'These are the creations of a madman. Should we wish to have the history of the empire written by a madman?'

Observing the willingness with which former Chinese officials and tutors agreed to collaborate on the historical work filled Poyun with disgust and bitter sarcasm.

They had been offered the bait and taken it.

But able to see the hook in the bait, he had held himself back and continued to swim in the sea of ink.

24

Sometimes a tightness gripped his chest. He felt both exuberant and deeply saddened, like a surging spring hemmed in by a rock, or a fire smothered by a wet blanket.

He had a dream.

He was lying on the petal of a giant lotus flower, a satiny, unshaded, fragrant surface. All at once this white carpet began to draw up at the edges until it formed a funnel. His body toppled and started rolling. As the petal goblet became steeper there was nothing he could hold on to, and he began to slip until he fell into a bowl. It was filled with black ink. The ink was warm, like his body, and he was not afraid, he felt secure in there. Now he dived into the dark liquid, closing his eyes and mouth. He did not gasp for air; the ink seemed to breathe for him.

It sucked him in, through a long, narrow channel only as wide as his body. Inside the flower stem he slid down until at some point he felt a soft pad absorb the ink like sand does water. It became ever brighter until he could make out a silver strip of light in the distance. Carried on a gentle black wave, he approached the light. He stroked his hand over the ground and felt the rough surface of paper.

Now he felt his body, too: he was wet and smooth. His skin had become scaly with a red shimmer. He tried to stand but his legs were missing. He had grown fins in their place and they stuck to the paper. He struggled to free them, but the struggling only stuck them more firmly to the paper.

He called out to a man who was walking past, 'I've become separated from my natural surroundings, I'm helpless. If I could just have a bucket of water, that would keep me alive!'

The man bent down towards him. He recognized the face of the government commissar who had brought him the imperial assignment to work on the great history. The man stroked his smooth belly to check how wet it was and then said, 'I'm on my way to the ink sea. I'm going to run a channel from there to here. So you'll be able to swim over. Is that all right with you, goldfish?'

'If you have your way, sir, you'll soon be finding me in the shop that sells dried fish!'

25 He and his wife became estranged. She found his mood swings and taciturnity intolerable, and went back to her family. He himself was in despair about his condition and he begged her not to spurn him. He lambasted her: 'You made a show of insisting how we should eat and sleep together. But over the past thirty days there have been twenty-nine when we have not. Every night leaves fall from the wutong tree and the seeds become increasingly meagre.'

She asked him why he danced and sobbed outside, and sometimes behaved skittishly only to fall back into silence again. Why was he away so often?

Suddenly she was afraid of him.

He painted a small picture of crab-apple blossom and wrote beneath it: *Your husband is just as good and bad as before. Why is there no harmony between you and him any longer? Why do you make plans to exchange him for a horse? Once we spoke of buying a pine wood on the other side of the Wu bridge and raising deer and making the best ink for all the world's pictures. Red flowers carpet the hillside, the spring streams caress the rocks. Like your love they open their flowers and then wither. The stream flows endlessly, like my sorrow.*

He sent her this picture after she had already left him. But she did not reply. He wrote to her once more: *On whom should the scent of the orchid model itself? I can no longer tell whether twilight belongs to the morning or the evening. Was it you who sent me these cawing ravens? I hate the pasture by the pavilion. I watch ants in the moss moving their nest. The sadness of the pines dripping in the rain and this wind which never stops blowing.*

But no word ever came back.

26 It was at this time that he first summoned the courage to hold his dead master's paintbrush. He set out a piece of paper and poured water into the hollow of the rubbing stone. He rubbed the ink and drenched the brush. Then he ran it over the peach stone until the bristles stopped dripping.

Starting in the bottom left-hand corner, he made a bold stroke across the entire width of the paper and then continued in a right angle upwards, slowly lifting his hand so that the line, after a slight curve to the left, finished in a point. Around this point he planted three deep-black, almost round blobs, inserting between these some delicate, parallel, wavy lines with the tip of the brush.

Above where the thick line at the bottom began, he now led the brush in a gently winding movement to the top, where he again finished the stroke with two blobs cut off by the edge of the paper. He added a few short spikes on either side of the three bold strokes by thrusting the tip of the brush into the black vein from about a finger's width away.

He wet the brush tip with ink a second time and signed the small piece of paper with the characters *ba da shan ren*. He had given himself another name: man on the mountain of the eight compass points.

He endorsed the picture with his seal.

When he fixed the picture to the wall to view it, he could see a fine forked branch at the end of which sat a rose in bloom.

Like an armed guard, the thorny branch defended the beauty at its tip. The seductive petals would soon fall, but the thorns would remain.

Branch of blossom with thorns

27 Since his second wife had left him, Bada Shanren had been leading the life of a vagabond. At the age of sixty he no longer had his own retreat; he was free from all ties.

He had renounced whatever would not fit into his paltry luggage. Everything else seemed superfluous.

Like a bird he drifted from place to place, whistling and singing, only ever settling down temporarily. He accepted all the hospitality extended to him. But often people were full of mistrust when they met him; they thought he was mad.

Wherever possible he stayed with friends.

When he met an old acquaintance he would make himself useful straight away and work for him all day long without a break. He pushed himself to the limit, forgetting all else as he did so.

This was how he lived.

28 From this time he used only the one name, Bada Shanren. He was asked about the meaning of the name and he would reply, 'The points of the compass symbolize the eight directions of space which each painter worthy of the title must be capable of opening up with a single brushstroke.'

Whenever he wrote the four characters of his name, *ba da shan ren*, he would put them together in such a way that they could be read not only as Bada Shanren, but also in another arrangement: as the characters *kuzhi* and *xiaozhi*, which mean the crying man and laughing man. He was the laughing man who also cried, and the crying man who laughed too. He could not merely cry or laugh; his laughter always contained a tear and he cried tears of laughter.

'Isn't it terrible to live with so much uncertainty and fear for the future?' he was asked by a friend who put him up for a while.

That same night Bada Shanren took out a piece of paper, rubbed some ink and lowered his brush into the hollow of the rubbing stone.

He painted a large dot somewhat to the right of the centre of the paper. Below this a short, flat line, to the side of that a similar vertical one, and above the dot a finely drawn arc the breadth of a fingertip. He left some space around these marks, then he painted a palm-sized area beside and below the two short lines by pressing the brush down onto the paper, rolling it on its axis and wiggling it to produce an irregular black patch whose edges, punctuated by individual bristles, had extremely fine points.

At the bottom of this ball of colour he drew a thin, horizontal line which extended as far as the vertical axis of the dot. Halfway along this line he added a second, equally thin but much shorter line, crossing the first one at a sharp angle.

In the left half of the picture, a little lower than the first dot, he now painted a second one which he likewise bordered with a line that he brought downwards in a gentle arc and then took to the right, almost horizontally. Where the line ended he applied the brush to the paper once more, leading it downwards diagonally and then, with a tilt of his hand, angling it slightly to the right. Through the resulting bend he painted a straight line downwards, bringing it to a point shortly after the intersection. Above the second dot he pressed the brush down onto the paper as before, extending the blotch that appeared upwards, eventually letting it fade to the side. An almost rectangular shape emerged above the dot, forming a slight overhang in the upper right corner.

Now he dipped his brush again and signed the paper with the characters *ba da shan ren*. Finally he printed his red seal on it. He presented the picture to his host, saying, 'Here you can see how I feel.'

'But that's two chicks,' his host said.

'Yes,' Bada replied, 'and there's an eagle circling above them, but that you can see only in the chicks' expressions. The bird of prey will swoop down on top of them, but they can share their fear and rely on their mother. I crossed the threshold and left my homeland long ago, and my heart trembles along the length of the path. I share my fear with my pictures alone.'

Two chicks

29 One day Bada Shanren was the guest of a goldfish breeder. He showed Bada around his garden, which he called the Garden of the Yellow Bamboo.

To Bada's great astonishment, his host did not mention goldfish once. He had made up his own lyrical names for all the shrubs and trees, and he enthused about their subtle colours and the variety of their leaf forms. Late in the afternoon he suddenly grabbed Bada's arm.

'This is the moment. Now the light is perfect.'

Bada was taken to the veranda behind the house. There, an assistant was standing a number of blue-and-white porcelain bowls on the low wall.

'Master,' the host said, 'please look at my fish. Look at them all and tell me which colour you like best!'

Bada looked one by one into all the bowls. He noticed that the goldfish breeder had arranged the fish in a colour scale. The first one was saffron yellow. The scales of the second glistened pink, the third and fourth were both bright orange. The fifth shone a lurid red, the sixth had a purple back. The final one seemed to him almost violet.

In each bowl was a single fish, almost the size of carp. They were so large that they could swim only in a tight circle, forced to bend their heavy bodies to the limit. It was clear that they noticed the change in light on the water when Bada bent over them. They looked at him through the clear water with their large round eyes and seemed to be trying to kiss the surface with their plump lips, shattering the delicate glass each time. The light glinted colourfully on their stout backs.

Bada chose the last fish, the violet one.

'Why the darkest one, Master?' the goldfish breeder asked with a hint of surprise.

'If I stood by the pond in the noonday sunlight and saw a school of your violet fish, I would be watching the night swimming in the water.'

30

After his visit to the goldfish breeder, Bada Shanren settled on the shore of a lake near the Orchid Temple and put himself up in an old fisherman's hut. He gave his modest abode the name Song after Waking, which he wrote on the wooden planks in large white characters.

When he had become familiar with his surroundings and had found peace again, he put a long roll of paper on his low painting table. To keep the paper flat he weighed it down with stones from the river. He rubbed ink and dipped his paintbrush.

In the upper left-hand corner of the picture he allowed a large, irregular shape to emerge, which in places he outlined with shading. Diagonally opposite, in the lower right-hand corner of the picture, he painted a second shape, similar to the first. Their contours seemed to snuggle up to each other across the wide space between. In this empty space Bada used the tip of his brush to paint a tiny arc, the upper end of which split into two prongs. Two hand widths away from this, set slightly below, he made a stroke across the paper which also divided on the right, but which was then rounded off by another delicate downwards stroke, thereby leaving a narrow empty space between the upper straight line and lower rounded one.

He painted four other objects of a similar shape and size, close to the outline of the large shape at the bottom.

To finish he signed his name, stamping his seal below it.

When the ink was dry he attached the roll of paper to one of the ceiling beams so that it caught the light

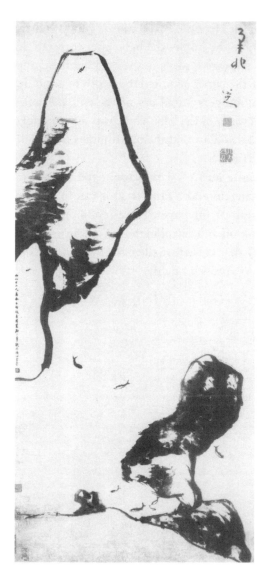

Fish and rocks

shining in. Here the black colour swallowed the sun's rays; there the ink let the light filter through and grey clouds appeared, while in the backlight the unpainted area of the paper acquired the depth of sand dunes.

Two boulders jutted out of the embankment above the still water of the lake. There was movement between the rocks and around them. Minnows darted about in the clear water.

A gentle gust of wind caught the picture hanging like a curtain and a faint tremor ran in a wave down the length of the paper. For a few moments the little fish took off and swam in the air. Their joy was for the eternity that lay before them. But no one was pressing them to express it openly.

31 Bada Shanren had become a master and young painters came from far and wide to show him their work and seek advice. They generally brought small gifts, ink tablets from their province or jars of jam, and he would thank them politely. These visits punctuated long periods of silence, when he would immerse himself completely in his work.

Bada looked patiently at the mountains and rivers, the pines, the bamboo, all the cranes and wild geese and fish. Everything seemed so superficial, so stiff and lifeless. A heap of bones and ashes. He would then give the painter the following advice: 'When you walk, do not think about walking, but let your feet dance on the soft forest floor. When you paint, do not think about painting, but let your wrist dance.'

Soon afterwards monks from the Monastery of the Green Cloud also visited him in his fisherman's hut.

Once he was sitting with a monk on the shore, speaking of the joys of being a fish.

'But Master, you're not a fish,' the monk countered. 'How can you know whether fish can be happy?'

'You are not me,' Bada replied. 'How can you know that I do not know when a fish is happy?'

'No, I'm not you,' the monk said. 'So I cannot know what's in your mind. But you are definitely not a fish. That is certain. So I doubt that you can know fish feel pleasure.'

'Let us start at the beginning once more,' Bada said. 'When you asked me how I could know what fish feel, you already knew that I know, and you asked me how. My answer to this is: I know, for the happiness I feel is not my own.'

32 Shao Changheng, man of letters and functionary, also harboured a strong desire to meet Bada Shanren. He had studied and admired the master's calligraphy, without ever being able to acquire any of his work.

When in 1688 Shao stayed as a guest of an abbot friend of his in the Orchid of the South Monastery near Nanchang, a well-informed monk was sent to the master's abode to request whether Shao might be able see him. The messenger returned the following day to say that the master agreed to meet Shao Changheng in the Orchid Temple.

When the appointed day arrived it was pouring with rain. With such bad weather Shao could not expect the ageing master to keep their engagement. In spite of his doubts, however, he called for a bamboo litter and set off.

He was only halfway to the temple when Bada came running to meet Shao, gave him a warm greeting and then burst out into loud laughter. Shao saw an old man of slight build with a faintly reddish face, sunken cheeks and a thin moustache whose ends hung down in fine strands. The man was wearing a fisherman's hat from which the rainwater dripped all around as if from a fountain. His shoes and cape were sopping wet, but this seemed not to trouble the man; he danced and sang alongside the litter on the final stretch to the monastery.

They spent half the night in conversation by lamplight. The master became less and less talkative, whereas his gestures became increasingly animated until his whole body moved with them.

All of a sudden Bada demanded some ink and a brush, which the monks gave him without delay. Now he started frenetically covering sheets of paper with calligraphy, writing dark words which Shao was unable to interpret. Bada went on in this frenzy until he collapsed from exhaustion and fell asleep on the spot.

Outside a violent storm was raging and water was swooshing from the gutters. Gusts of wind rattled the windows and doors, and around the pavilion the bamboo groaned like tigers in the deserted mountains.

There was such commotion that night that Shao could not sleep. He was overcome by an interminable sorrow, like black water flowing into an empty lake basin. He would have liked to wake the master and shed tears with him, but such things were beyond him, and he merely felt sadder as a result.

He was unable to sleep because he felt more awake than in the daytime, more awake than he had ever felt.

As the storm continued to rage, Bada remained motionless, like a drowned man.

Shao became worried and bent over him.

Bada was fast asleep, with a cheerful expression on his face.

33

Later, in summer, another young painter visited the master, asking many questions and seeking advice.

'How can I develop my own style?' the painter wanted to know.

'Originality!' Bada laughed. 'I am as I am, I paint as I paint. I have no method, I do not think about originality, I am just me.'

'But surely I have to choose the style of the Northern or Southern School.'

'You come from no school and you go to no school. The school does not come to you, either, and no school goes forth from you. Take a brush and some ink and simply paint your own style.'

Bada could see the young man's questioning look. So he elucidated further: 'We do not know which style the ancients followed before developing their own painting style. And when it had reached maturity they did not allow their successors to renounce this style. For centuries their successors were unable to lift their heads from the ground. Like those who follow in the footprints of the ancients rather than following their own hearts. A truly lamentable state of affairs, it means a young painter becomes the slave of another, well-known painter. Apart from that, avoid flatness, excess detail and, most of all, continuing with a well-worn pattern. What is painting if not the technique of the universe's changes and developments?'

'Does that mean I don't have to begin with the role models and attain their level of expertise before striking my own path?' the pupil asked.

'When you talk like that you are forgetting that besides the old role models you also have your own: yourself. You cannot hang on to the beards of the ancients. You must try to be your own life and not the death of another. For this reason the best painting method is the method of no method. Even if the brush, the ink, the drawing are all wrong, what constitutes your "I" still survives. You must not let the brush control you; you must control the brush yourself.'

34

Bada Shanren had been invited by the abbot to the Orchid Temple. They drank their fill of liquor and laughed into the summer night. The following day Bada took leave of his host very early and set off on his way back to the fisherman's hut where he still lived.

A fine rain had set in. Bada wandered through the pine forest beneath the monastery and breathed in the fragrance, for the damp trees were letting off an aroma. Amidst the silence he told himself, 'You must know when the world acquired you and when the time has come to leave it. My life is fading away like the magnificence of the cherry blossom in the rain, and I feel only sadness at the emptiness which remains. I have filled it with my signs, but have I thereby proved my existence?'

He stopped. 'Is this a suicidal thought? Or is it quite the opposite? Why does the rain have this effect on me? Surely there is nothing softer in the world than water. And surely nothing better for softening hard and severe things.'

He was approaching his dwelling. He saw the hut by the lake, squatting at the foot of the mountain, and he stopped again to savour the view.

The trees, the rocks, the mountain stream in the rain.

Everything seemed blurred and other-worldly. Everything playing out incessantly before him – was it merely the flow of things? Was it the trees dripping in the mist which made the world appear like that, or was it the tears in his eyes?

No sooner was he back in his abode than he took a large piece of paper and wiped it with the wet sleeve of his robe. He hurriedly poured water into the rubbing stone and prepared the ink.

Beginning halfway down, his gleaming black brush drew five parallel lines at variable intervals from the left-hand edge of the paper, an area which was barely damp. He then added seven vertical and diagonal strokes until the outline of his hut was recognizable, though half of it was cut off by the paper's margin.

He took the brush with the cropped bristles. He turned it several times in the ink and guided it down the length of the still-moist paper, now using just the side, now pressing it down like a scrubbing brush, twisting it slightly before lifting the brush at the bottom of the paper. He thus painted a succession of column-like light and dark grey shapes which blended fluidly into one another as the damp paper dissolved the contours.

His tiny house, however, stood clearly and solidly on the mountainside, its back turned to the lamenting world and the desolate mountain behind a curtain of rain.

Fine streams of ink ran down the mountain; indeed the entire mountain seemed to flow away as if it were nothing more than a large wound of the world.

He wrote his name on the picture and added the date: *Painted on the night of the 27th day of the ninth month.* He did not put the year. His pictures did not exist in the calendar of the new dynasty.

Landscape with hut

35 Some years had passed since that September night. Bada Shanren had reached the age of seventy. He addressed a letter to a friend in which he described his daily routine: *I have a clean table beneath a light window. I read the ideas of dead masters from a past dynasty. I close the book and light an incense stick while contemplating what I have read. When I feel I have understood something I am happy and I smile to myself. With a brush and some ink I express my thoughts and empty my mind. An important guest arrives, but we put formalities aside. I make some green tea and together we enjoy the wonderful poems he has brought with him. After a while, deep yellow rays from the evening sun illuminate the room, and in the door frame I can see the rising moon. The visitor leaves and crosses the stream which flows into the lake by my house. Then I close the door and lie down on my mat. Lying on my back, I watch the moon through the window. I remain lying there, motionless, feeling carefree and content. I listen to the sound of a solitary cricket. Who is outside composing an elegy for me? My thoughts are carried far away.*

36 It was spring. Bada Shanren was sitting on a narrow veranda, thinking of his wife. Where might she be now?

Despite the sun it was raining heavily.

The embankment was a pale green.

A pair of herons flew past, brushing the weeping willow.

A swim, then joyful leaps in the naked light.

The curtain of rain lifted, the view extended as far as the jade horizon, along lathe-turned balustrades of cloud without end.

The water in the lake mirrored the fading sky, the trees held the fog like censers, gradually allowing the eye to make out their forms once more.

Bada was absorbed by the distant view to the south.

This tiny heart, he thought, and eyes which gaze into the infinite.

And he could hardly tell whether he was painting this picture in his mind or whether he was really looking at it.

He waited and observed every change. The clouds looked so dense, it seemed as if he could carve great blocks out of them.

He imagined a house in the sky built from blocks of cloud.

37 As the years passed, life in isolation became too arduous. Bada Shanren decided to return to his home city of Nanchang.

He rented a shabby room in Xifumen, a poor area in the southern part of the city.

Tall plants covered the façade, coiling around doors and windows and darkening the room.

Bada liked these plants; he wanted to live beside them and so moved in, even though the houses were desolate and run-down.

The room was in a wretched condition: the window frames were rotten and everything was thick with dust.

But he had immersed himself so deeply into the spirit of Chan that his external surroundings were practically immaterial.

The dust and lack of light could not impair his brushes.

38 He did not remove the spiders which had made themselves at home in all corners of his room. In the morning, when sunlight fell through the windows, the spiders' webs caught the rays and he could make out every single thread. In the evenings the threads became lost again in the dimness and the spiders' bodies seemed to float in the room like black dots.

How easily I could squash them, Bada thought.

If, in the mornings, he saw the little spider waiting stock-still in the middle of its web above the window, he felt as blissful as a child. It waited as if this waiting could end at any moment, if a fat housefly got caught in the web.

But that seldom happened.

One day he noticed that the right-hand side of the web by the window was torn and the spider was missing, too. Was this due to the night-time storm?

Later, however, the spider reappeared. It was busy weaving a new web, a bit further to the right and also closer to the window frame, leaving a small space between the new web and what remained of the old one.

Unable to take his eyes off the spider, Bada watched the slow process of spinning a web. But now he saw that it must be another spider creating this web, as industrious little legs were crawling again around the shredded rigging of the old, slightly higher one. Surely this was the old spider returning to assess the damage to its web.

How horrified it must be! A fellow member of its species had turned up, no doubt ready to net the entire supply of flies in this corner with a new web. The second spider moved straight to the centre of its web, awaiting in irritation the approaches of the first.

When the first spider likewise reached the centre of its web, still intact, it was thus confronted by another, only a few body lengths away, which had already spun its own web. The spiders no longer seemed to be waiting for flies, only for the next move their rival was going to make. But neither stirred. Merely the faintest of quivers ran down their thin legs onto the threads.

Bada looked away and excitedly prepared to paint. He placed a small, square leaf of paper from his album on the table and rubbed some ink. He wet the brush and smoothed it on the peach stone to make the tip as fine as possible.

One finger length above the centre of the page and a little to the left, he very carefully drew the fine outline of a spider, about the size of his thumbnail, two minute dots as eyes and, radiating from the centre of the body, four pairs of legs that mirrored each other. The tips of these eight legs together described an exact circle. The insect's body pointed to the lower right-hand corner of the paper.

Below this spider and a touch to the right he now drew a second spider whose body was oriented so that the line of its axis crossed that of the first spider in the centre of the paper. All that distinguished the second spider from the first was that its back right leg was at an angle rather than stretched out, hinting that it would be likely to make the next move.

Two spiders

Bada had drawn no webs, only spiders' bodies with outspread legs the width of a hair, yet a fine network of silver threads appeared to span the picture.

But neither the first nor the second spider sat in the centre of *this* web, for it was the centre of the paper. An invisible spider sat there, mesmerizing the eye and spinning a web of meaning across the whole picture.

Neither of the two spiders could compete with the third. They did not see it. All they noticed was that the centres of their webs were too close to each another. They would never reach the spot where their paths intersected.

And so they were frozen in perpetual anticipation.

39 Bada Shanren received a letter from someone who signed his name as Shitao. The man wrote that he had been born in the province of Guangxi. When he was three years old his father, the Prince of Jingjiang, had died in an internal power struggle between the last Mings. His father was a descendant of the eldest brother of the founder of the Ming dynasty. He and Bada were thus distant relatives.

After his father's death he had lived in anonymity for many years, Shitao wrote. He had called himself The Survivor of Jingjiang. Eventually he had entered a Buddhist monastery, where he gave himself the name Monk with the Gourd. In the monastery he had started painting with ink. Many years later he had abruptly left. For a time now he had been living as a vagabond in the southerly provinces.

I have many existences, but in painting I am always myself, he wrote.

Then Shitao addressed Bada: *In Yangzhou, the artistic and economic centre of our age, I had the opportunity to discover your work. This induced me to write and make contact with you.*

Bada read on: *Master Shanren, your paintings and calligraphy are the greatest and most accomplished I know. Your pictures exist for eternity. Under many different names they are in circulation or in the possession of fools, but I am one of the few who know they were all painted by the same hand which now holds this piece of paper. It was a monk who confided in me, a monk who had been under the tutelage of Abbot Hongmin and who could not stop talking about you. If this letter ever reaches you, stick it to your door so that those who pass by can read it and learn just how great a master lives amongst them. For my sake I beg you to do me this favour. Your admirer and cousin, the humble Shitao.*

Bada did not like attracting people's attention and having his peace disturbed. But he did as the letter-writer wished and stuck Shitao's letter outside on the door to his home.

And, in fact, some passers-by did stop briefly. But they could not understand how the master this letter talked about could live in such poor circumstances, and so thought the whole thing was the self-glorification of a harmless old man who had gone a little mad.

40 Bada Shanren thought it great serendipity when a fellow traveller from a past he had believed dead and buried turned up out of the blue, as if somewhere a huge eye were looking out for people who belonged together, ensuring that their paths crossed.

He had forgotten the dustiness and sparseness of his lodging; ever more his thoughts took him back to the fisherman's hut, to the water.

A fine rain was falling, then the sun broke through again. The wet branches and rocks glistened. The mountains shimmered blue, birds flew down onto the hut and sang. He awoke, went outside onto the dewy grass and sang with them.

Still immersed in past pictures, he rolled out the paper on the low table. He filled the hollow of the rubbing stone and rubbed some ink. He blackened the brush and wiped it across the curve of the peach stone until it no longer dripped.

With quick, unerring strokes he made a slender fish appear from the white surface in the upper third of the long rectangle. Five small blobs sufficed to give it fins. He inked in its back and tail fins, leaving the belly white. He painted a dot in a small oval.

That was the fish's eye.

He filled the bottom third of the paper with the round contours of a rock, the form of which was cut off by the bottom right corner of the paper. With a few broad and firm, slightly curved strokes of the brush, he gave the boulder depth.

On the rock he placed a bird that had turned its

head around and was resting its heavy beak on its back feathers. He suggested the two halves of the beak with a line which he drew back, gently curving it upwards beneath the eye, so that the bird appeared to be smiling.

The bird's eye was no different from that of the fish. But the fish's gaze was lost somewhere beyond the paper's margin, where nothing was to be seen, whereas the raven held in its gaze the fish floating above. Or was it a duck? Or was the raven watching the fish swimming below?

Finally he signed the paper with the characters that denoted his name. For this he used the upper left corner of the paper. Lower down, by the edge, he put his seal.

Now the characters *ba da shan ren* sat directly in the fish's sights. So something had caught the attention of its eye after all – it was no longer looking into nothingness, but at a man on the mountain of the eight compass points.

Bird, fish, rock

41 One morning Bada Shanren heard a knocking at his door. Opening it, he saw before him a man with fine facial features wearing an expensive robe. The stranger greeted him with exceptional politeness.

'Master Bada? My name is Fang Shihuan, I'm an art agent from Yangzhou. I have just read the letter on your door written by the great Shitao. I knew, therefore, that I had found my life's goal!'

Without saying a word, Bada made tea for his guest.

They sat on the cushions on the floor.

Bada did not ask whether his cousin Shitao had sent the man here. In any event it was virtually impossible to ask questions, for Fang spoke like a waterfall.

'Master,' he said, 'so many famous collectors and art-lovers have approached me to enquire about works by your hand. Should I be permitted to represent you as your agent, my greatest wish would come true!'

Bada asked him to remain sitting.

He opened the sandalwood boxes and took out his collection of loose-leaf albums. He put the pictures on the mat in front of the art dealer, one after the other.

Fang Shihuan's eyes shone.

Not another word passed his lips.

42 Bada Shanren was sitting beside a blank piece of paper, his brush at the ready, and was about to start – but he was held captive by one thought.

How can it be that, from a dismal sky, this bitter world can suddenly show us that we love it, in spite of everything; and that in spite of everything it will be hard to take our leave of it? We cannot embark on the journey of death by ourselves, but perhaps the sum of the wise man's learning lies in the decision to go, to set off, to leave.

With determination he dipped the brush into the well of ink and wrote on the paper in one flowing movement: *I will go into the mountains, where the trees are old and withered as I am, and the ravines will rise up into the emptiness.*

Then, on the piece of paper next to it he drew a mule in simple lines. On its back crouched a man with a broad-brimmed hat.

Bada took a clean brush, dipped it into a bowl of clear water and wet the paper around the figure of the rider.

He returned to the brush with ink. Holding it just above the paper, he squeezed out the ink with two fingers of his left hand. It dripped onto the damp paper, where it quickly spread.

Now he took the brush with the cropped bristles, which was as spiky as a broom. He rubbed it on a tablet of ink that he had moistened lightly. With jittery movements he smeared it across the paper. What appeared were the outlines of a path, a tall tree and some branches.

Landscape with rider

The mule was leading its rider into a hazy bank of fog. The good beast had turned its head to the side. Its ears were pricked up. It was staring with large wide eyes at Bada, who had painted it. The world is behind us, but what kind of dream are we riding into, O sunken one? When shall I carry you?

43 Many months had passed when he was handed a letter by a stranger who said he was a friend of Shitao's. He read: *Cousin Bada, I have kept your letter. I have not answered before now as I've been ill. The same goes for letters I've received from other people. Today a friend is returning to Nanchang. I have asked him to bring you this letter, with which I've enclosed a small picture. The picture shows the Pavilion of Great Clarity on the bank of a river, surrounded by trees. In the upper half sits an old man in the middle of a bare rock. There is still space on the paper. Would you please add a few words? For me the picture would then be – how should I put it? – indispensable. It would be the most valued treasure in my possession.*

Bada Shanren unrolled the enclosed picture and studied it for a while. Then he read on: *From everything that I've heard, it seems as if you are still skipping up mountains, in spite of your seventy-four or seventy-five years. You are like an immortal! As for me, Zhu Da, I am close to sixty and no longer able to undertake any major activity.*

Bada put down the letter, reached for the ink and rubbing stone and took hold of his brush.

He completed the picture with a little waterfall and leaves that emphasized the autumnal mood. Then he painted the following words in the remaining blank space: *Above the Pavilion of Great Clarity bright clouds are opening, infinitely high, as the new register of immortals is carried from the violet chamber. The sky has already unfurled its wings and nothing of the old dust and muck remains in the world.*

When the picture was dry he rolled it up and gave it to a messenger who would be sure to get to Shitao at some point.

44

Nobles and rich men everywhere began to venerate the creations of his brush. He received invitations and was easily persuaded when good wine was promised.

Naturally the hosts anticipated that, once sufficiently lubricated and in the right mood, Bada Shanren would reach for his brush and leave behind a magnificent ink drawing. So long as Bada was sober, any collector after even just a page from an album with a few drawings would not get a thing. They could place a gold bar under Bada's nose and still have no success. Thus these people tried other ways of acquiring his pictures, such as pretending they were not keen on his work.

When one evening he was invited to what he thought would be a perfectly harmless drinking session, next to his seat Bada found a bucket full of ink and endless rolls of paper. Paintbrushes of all sizes hung down from the ceiling within his reach.

To begin with he ignored the equipment. They drank lots of wine, laughed, slapped their thighs. He forgot himself.

But much later in the evening one of the men present, who was said to be a famous actor, took the largest brush and started caressing it as if he were stroking his lover's hair. The brush was the size of a broom and he held it upside down, singing to it in a deep, rattling voice.

His short performance received a boisterous round of applause. Then Bada leapt to his feet and grabbed the brush from the actor. He lowered it deep into the tub, stirring the paint as if it were soup. The host, inwardly delighted, at once fetched one of the rolls of paper and, with the help of some other guests, now put four or five lengths of paper beside one another, carpeting the entire floor.

A mixture of singing and shouting struck up when Bada moved to the middle of the room with the heavy, dripping brush. Now he started, slowly at first, then ever faster, turning around so that the ink flowing from the brush formed a fine compass circle. When the brush had finished dripping, Bada stepped out of the black ring and painted the area of the circle as if he were sweeping a small manège with a broom. In the light of the lanterns the wet ink glistened like varnish.

He immediately painted a second round island next to the first, although as he turned around this time he let the brush tip glide over the paper before filling in the shape with black ink. He continued to paint nothing but circles, some large, some small, one after the other, all of them touching but never overlapping. Gradually the white areas of the paper looked like four-pronged shapes made of curved lines only.

When he had covered all the paper with black balls he hung the brush back on the beam and proclaimed, 'A sky full of stars.'

But no sooner had he uttered these words than he unexpectedly seized the bucket, which was still half full, and poured the rest of the ink over the paper. It was not long before he had smeared and rubbed the remaining white patches black with his sandals, emitting horrible cries all the while. Some of the guests jumped up and grabbed him by the arm and chest, but Bada shook them off and his voice resounded through the throng of hands: 'Look, look, the black stars in the black sky! The darkness is a universe!'

45 He was astonished when one day he received a reply from his cousin Shitao, in which the latter expressed his gratitude for Bada's words above the picture of the hermit. The letter was accompanied by a small roll of paper. *The picture I have sent you is called* A thousand wild dashes of ink, Shitao wrote. *They are the traces of my brush, which I let dance over the paper in delight at your words. I really ought to have painted an orchid or bamboo or a heron, but that would have been like trying to hold a candle to the master. These modest dashes, however, are the genesis of all these things, the joy of the brush. Will we ever meet?*

Bada unrolled the picture and let it work on his soul. Dots of ink were connected by fine diagonal lines. The overall pattern looked like the traces of bark beetles on bare wood. In between were coral shapes with nodes or a pattern of just ovals. The only larger coherent mass of colour was at the left-hand margin, consisting of lumpy shapes with very fine branchwork.

When Bada stuck the rolled-out picture to the wall and viewed it from the other side of the room, it had changed. It no longer looked just like a collection of apparently meaningless dots, lines and blobs, but like a section of a garden in bloom with boughs full of fruit, luxuriant round shrubs, wild orchids, a squat, withered tree trunk and branches spread out wide with fine petals.

He could not help laughing.

His cousin had almost put one over on him.

46

Over time Bada was a less frequent visitor to drinking sessions, and after a few years he even kept his distance from them altogether.

With each year that he got older, he found the present less important and flat. Memories of events that lay far back in the past popped up in his mind. He tried to recall how, as a young man, he had thought about the world. He remembered his father's eyes and his lips, which moved without a word ever falling from them – the father who he always understood nonetheless.

It was the first time he had gone weeks without painting. Instead he sat in a corner almost motionless for hours, buried in his thoughts.

He suddenly remembered the balls of ink that Abbot Hongmin had given him. He had never touched them. He found them straight away in a casket. Now he rubbed, for the very first time, the ink of the great ink-maker, Pan Gu. Then he set out a small piece of paper and dipped his brush.

In the centre of the paper he painted a fish from the side, with a shimmering violet back and a silver belly, the tail fins almost semicircular like the bristles of a dry paintbrush. The fish's mouth was half open, as if it were about to say something. Its left eye peered up to the edge of the paper with an expression combining fear, suspicion, detachment and scorn.

The eye was a small black dot stuck to the upper arc of the oval surrounding it.

The fish swam from right to left across the paper.

Bada painted this one fish and no other, then put his name to the paper.

He had perished long ago, but he was still alive. All he feared now was the drought, when the ink no longer flowed and life had been worn down to nothing.

That is how he saw himself.

Fish

47 As rubbing the ink was increasingly becoming a strain, Bada would sometimes just make movements with the dry brush.

And yet he painted every day, even if no pictures were produced.

He was not yet satisfied with his art; he wanted finally to do away with the chattiness of his earlier pictures.

Now he used only Pan Gu's ink, albeit very thriftily.

How many more strokes could he manage before the last of the ink had been worn away? Innumerable?

Truly, he thought, it is no mere empty saying that ink wears the man down and not the other way round.

Deep night, the oil lamp was smoking.

The sound of heavy rain, the wind rattling the window.

He could not find sleep. He thought of the fine, polished jade clasps in his wife's hair.

Why did this memory never grow old?

48

Or he would dip the brush into a bowl with clean water and paint invisible figures on the paper.

He had set himself one final goal.

He wanted to paint flowing water.

For hours he practised with only the brush and no ink, until his arm hurt. He began in the upper right-hand corner, bringing the paintbrush downwards and describing a long curve to the left while reducing the pressure on the brush. Then he let the stroke peter out by slowly lifting the brush and drawing it towards his chest. At the point where the line turned to the left he started a second line which he took downwards, veering slightly to the right, then let it run parallel to, and below, the course of the first one, before joining the end of both strokes with a semicircle.

When he had taught his hand these three movements, he put down his brush and for several days carried them out just using his fingers on the blank paper.

He spread out many pieces of paper on his desk. At night, in the darkness, he dipped the tip of his middle finger into a bath of ink and let his finger execute the three curved strokes, without being able to see the traces of ink in the darkness.

He continued like this all night long.

When the first light of morning lit up the desk, a shoal of fish appeared which vanished into the depths of the room.

A feeling of great calm flowed through Bada. Slower than ever, he rubbed the ink in the water until he had the right degree of blackness. He dipped the paintbrush and wiped the drops of ink on the peach stone. He closed his eyes and executed the strokes several times over in his mind before putting brush to paper.

Finally, his eyes still half closed in deep concentration, from his wrist he let the brush paint a curve to the left, starting as a broad and watery line because of the pressure he applied, then becoming thinner as he lifted the brush. He went over this curve again, just a touch below, and at the end of the first brushstroke he inserted a dash in the form of a pointed sail and, where the second line ran out, a small crescent whose concave side arched to the left.

From the lower point of the crescent he drew two parallel semicircles, one just below the other, reaching to the end of the higher first line. Finally he shaded the narrow white strip between the two semicircles and planted two fat dots to the right and left of the inner edge of the curve.

It had all happened in a few seconds.

Then he put his brush aside, stuck the picture on the wall, and wandered out of the city, up a mountain.

He recalled the master's words.

If the hand is supple and agile, the picture will be too, and it will move in various directions. The picture does not only show the movement of your hand, it is a reflection of its dance. If the hand moves with speed, the picture acquires vitality; if it moves slowly, the picture acquires weight and intensity. The brush guided by a hand of great talent creates things that the mind cannot follow, which transcend it. And if the wrist moves with the spirit, the hills and streams reveal their soul.

Catfish

When he returned that evening from his walk, the catfish on the wall looked at him with its tiny eyes.

Bada saw the water and all of a sudden his hand seemed to be a fin.

49 The following day he sat down and wrote a letter to his long-dead master: *Today, Master, I, Bada Shanren, sit here trying to ask myself what lesson I still need to learn, a question I have shied away from answering. My answer is: the lesson of the first stroke. For is the whole drawing not contained in the first stroke? It must be considered long in advance, perhaps a whole life long, in order to bring it to the paper in one fluid movement at the right moment, without the need or ability to correct it. The first brushstroke is the foundation; it is the internal law of the external movement. All other strokes take care of themselves, so to speak. The interrupted flow of the black ink, the suspended movement, everything visible and palpable arises from this. Stones and pools, rivers, waterfalls and mountains, lotus flowers, roses, orchids, fuchsias, chrysanthemums and pines, bamboo, cedars, chicks, crows, eagles and fish. Substance, fragrance, vitality, softness, noise, weather, thought and feeling. All this is in the line. But the initial stroke is the most important thing of all. That is my answer. Do you accept it?*

50 Bada's right hand had become so weak and tired that he could barely hold the paintbrush any more. Now he was ready to set off on his final journey, without any luggage. Without brush and without ink.

When the last of his strength was relentlessly vanishing, he reached for his brush once more and opened the little pot containing ready-made ink.

With a clammy hand he dipped the brush.

The brush tip approached the paper.

One final, delicate caress of the paper, so soft as if he were dabbing the wings of a butterfly with ink.

His eyes closed. For a moment he could still see the darkness beneath his eyelids, then he lowered his head onto the pillow.

The paintbrush slipped from his hand and fell onto his white shirt. It rolled slowly across his chest, leaving a black trail. The material soaked up the liquid and the stain spread rapidly.

A tiny black star shone in the room in all directions of the compass.

51

.

Afterword

Supposedly, the chronicles of the Monastery of the Green Cloud noted that its founder, Zhu Da, died in 1705 at the age of eighty. Apart from the years of his birth and death, little is known about the life of the Prince of Yiyang, who turned himself into the painter Bada Shanren. The few contemporary reports that exist speak of his madness; current research tends to take the view that he consciously manipulated his behaviour to avoid being co-opted by the hated regime. If Zhu Da was at the centre of one dynasty, he fell out of the frame of the succeeding one. Here I have told Zhu Da's life story alongside the biographical information and anecdotes that have been handed down, but the narrative is my invention. Moreover, the account is not as broad as it might have been because I have neglected the work of Bada the poet. Today there are 179 dated pictures and albums with paintings and calligraphy by Bada Shanren. They show mountains, forests and rivers, many species of plants, birds and fish – and yet they always seem to be self-portraits. *Sea of Ink* is an attempt to get inside the paintings, to tease out their words, to let them talk.

I should like to thank Tom Lawton, former director of the Freer and Sackler Galleries at the Smithsonian Institution, Washington, DC, for the tantalizing private view of scroll paintings and pages from albums in the museum's basement. Thanks are also due to Alexandra von Przychowski at the Rietberg Museum in Zürich for her help; and also to my brother Hugo K. Weihe for the scroll painting he gave me years ago: a bird sitting contentedly on an apple. Or is it a pumpkin? And why is the bird sitting on it as if on an egg? Is it trying to hatch all possible meanings? The picture is by Bada Shanren and actually the bird is sitting on an enigma in the form of an identifiable object. It was this that aroused my curiosity.

Richard Weihe

Notes on Sources

In several places I have made use of François Cheng's monograph *Chu Ta (1626–1705): Le génie du trait* (Paris: Phébus, 1986) and his sensitive introduction to Bada's visual imagery. In Chapter 21, for example, I have adopted the historically documented usage of metaphorical names for various brushstrokes. Cheng cites a short poem by Liu Yuxi (772–842), which I have worked into Chapter 25. In the description of the picture in Chapter 28 I use a quatrain by the poet Fei Sihuang from the eighteenth century, and in Chapter 36 some lines of verse from Wei Zhuang (836–910). A letter cited in full from Shitao to Bada Shanren served as the model for the letter in Chapter 43. For the description in Chapter 26 I have used Cheng's interpretation of the thorns as *'sentinelles armées et vigilantes de la beauté'*. My description of the picture in Chapter 30 (*Fish and rocks*) also contains an idea from Cheng – '*Mais rien ne les presse à vrai dire: leur amitié a toute l'éternité devant elle*' – while in Chapter 34 I have used his question in parentheses '*Arbres et rochers, voilés par le rideau de la pluie (ou par celui des larmes?) sont comme un geste d'adieu*' as a starting point for my interpretation of the picture of the cut-off house. Chapter 42 contains a literal quotation from Cheng. '*Savoir partir: toute la science du sage,*' he writes, and then asks, '*D'où vient pourtant que ce monde amer à tel point sache se faire aimer, à tel point soit dur à quitter?*'

Wang Fangyu and Richard M. Barnhart's catalogue of the exhibition *Master of the Lotus Garden: The Life and Art of Bada Shanren 1626–1705* (New Haven, Connecticut: Yale University Art Gallery, 1990) is the first comprehensive inventory of Bada Shanren's work. In Chapter 25 I use some lines from one of Bada's poems which Wang Fangyu cites in English. The translation of another original text, meanwhile, served as the basis for the letter in Chapter 35.

In his essay 'Zur Biographie des Pa-ta shan-jen' in *Asiatica: Festschrift Friedrich Weller zum 65. Geburtstag* (Leipzig: Otto Harrassowitz, 1954), pp. 119–30, Herbert Franke has assembled historical documents in German translation relating to the life of Bada Shanren. In Chapter 32 I use excerpts from Shao Zhangheng's recollections of a meeting with Bada. Chen Ting's outline of Bada's life has been an indispensable source, particularly his information about Bada's madness and the various names he gave himself. Herbert Franke also provides translations of the most important passages from Chinese treatises on ink in his book *Kulturgeschichtliches über die chinesische Tusche* (Munich: Bayerische Akademie der Wissenschaften, 1962). This source provided the background necessary for Chapter 16, as well as assisting other places in the text.

I have allowed Bada Shanren himself or his teacher, Master Hongmin, to utter some of the theses from Shitao's discourse on painting – 'Shih-t'ao: Quotes on Painting' in *Aesthetics: The Classic Readings*, edited by David E. Cooper (Oxford: Blackwell Publishers, 1997), pp. 65–76. In Chapter 33, therefore, we have Shitao's third thesis, which states that the best technique of painting is the 'technique of no technique'. The fourth thesis, in which Shitao describes the painting process as a step-by-step transfer of the idea of the picture onto the paper via the wrist, the brush and the ink, has made its way into Chapter 15, in association with ideas on the function of ink, paintbrush and the subject of the painting from thesis 18. The sublime significance of the function of water, taken from the same thesis, also crops up in Chapter 22.

The father's sentence from Chapter 4, 'A path comes into existence by being walked on', is a saying taken from the work of the fourth-century-BC philosopher Zhuang Zhou, more specifically from the following edition: *Zhuangzi – Das klassische Buch daoistischer Weisheit*, edited and with a commentary by Victor H. Maier, translated from the English by Stephan Schumacher (Frankfurt am Main: Krüger, 1998). The question which concludes Chapter 7 is also taken from this work. The idea developed in Chapter 15 of a unity of different things takes up one of Zhuangzi's central theories: 'This is also that, and that is also this.'

The dream meeting at the end of Chapter 24 cites a short extract from the anecdote about the goldfish, while the brief dialogue about the joy of fish is my amended version of a conversation between Master Zhuang and Master Hui.

Picture credits

Lotus flower
Page from an album, between 1689–92.

Ink on paper. Private collection, China. Photograph: all rights reserved.

Calamus
Page from an album with eleven leaves, around 1681.

Ink on paper, 30.2 x 34 cm. Princeton University Art Museum. Gift of Mrs George Rowley in memory of Professor George Rowley. Photograph © Bruce M. White.

Branch of blossom with thorns
Page from an album.

Ink on paper. Private collection, China. Photograph: all rights reserved.

Two chicks
Page from an album with sixteen leaves, in places dated 23/24 June 1693.

Ink on paper. Shanghai Museum. Photograph: all rights reserved.

Fish and rocks
Hanging scroll, dated 1696.

Ink on paper, 134.6 x 60.6 cm. Bequest of John M. Crawford Jr, 1988, © The Metropolitan Museum of Art, New York, all rights reserved.

Landscape with hut
Page from an album with twelve leaves, dated 1699.

Ink and light colour on paper, 23.3 x 16.8 cm. Bequest of John M. Crawford Jr, 1988, © The Metropolitan Museum of Art, New York, all rights reserved.

Two spiders
Page from an album with three leaves, dated 1691.

Ink on paper, 34.5 x 27.1 cm. Wang Fangyu and Sum Wai Collection. Reproduced with the kind permission of the Fred Fangyu Wang bequest.

Bird, fish, rock
Hanging scroll, dated 1694.

Ink on paper, 127.5 x 36.5 cm. Charles A. Drenowatz Collection, Museum Rietberg, Zürich. Photograph © Wettstein & Kauf.

Landscape with rider
Page from an album with twelve leaves, dated 21 December 1699.

Ink and light colour on paper, 21.3 x 16.8 cm. Bequest of John M. Crawford Jr, 1988, © The Metropolitan Museum of Art, New York, all rights reserved.

Fish
Page from an album with twenty-two leaves, in places dated 1694 and 1702 (The Anwan Album).

Ink on paper. Sumitomo Collection, Sen-oku Hakuko Kan, Kyoto, Japan.

Catfish
Page from an album with nine leaves, dated Spring 1691.

Ink on paper. Private collection, China. Photograph: all rights reserved.

Peirene

Contemporary
European Literature.
Thought provoking,
well designed, short.

*'Two-hour books to be
devoured in a single sitting:
literary cinema for those
fatigued by film.'* TLS

Online Bookshop

Subscriptions

Literary Salons

Reading Guides

Publisher's Blog

www.peirenepress.com

Follow us on twitter and Facebook @PeirenePress
Peirene Press is building a community of passionate readers.
We love to hear your comments and ideas.
Please email the publisher at: meike.ziervogel@peirenepress.com

Subscribe

Peirene Press publishes series of world-class contemporary novellas. An annual subscription consists of three books chosen from across the world connected by a single theme.

The books will be sent out in December (in time for Christmas), May and September. Any title in the series already in print when you order will be posted immediately.

The perfect way for book lovers to collect all the Peirene titles.

'A class act.' GUARDIAN

'An invaluable contribution to our cultural life.'
ANDREW MOTION

£35   1 Year Subscription (3 books, free p&p)

£65   2 Year Subscription (6 books, free p&p)

£90   3 Year Subscription (9 books, free p&p)

Peirene Press, 17 Cheverton Road, London N19 3BB
T 020 7686 1941
E subscriptions@peirenepress.com

www.peirenepress.com/shop
with secure online ordering facility

Peirene's Series

SMALL EPIC: UNRAVELLING SECRETS

NO 7

The Brothers by Asko Sahlberg

Translated from the Finnish by Emily Jeremiah and Fleur Jeremiah

'Intensely visual.' INDEPENDENT ON SUNDAY

NO 8

The Murder of Halland by Pia Juul

Translated from the Danish by Martin Aitken

'A brilliantly drawn character.' TLS

NO 9

Sea of Ink by Richard Weihe

Translated from the Swiss German by Jamie Bulloch

'Delicate and moving.' INDEPENDENT

....

TURNING POINT:
REVOLUTIONARY MOMENTS

NO 10

The Mussel Feast by Birgit Vanderbeke

Translated from the German by Jamie Bulloch

'An extraordinary book.' STANDPOINT

NO 11

Mr Darwin's Gardener by Kristina Carlson

Translated from the Finnish by Emily Jeremiah and Fleur Jeremiah

'Something miraculous.' GUARDIAN

NO 12

Chasing the King of Hearts by Hanna Krall

Translated from the Polish by Philip Boehm

'A remarkable find.' SUNDAY TIMES

COMING–OF–AGE: TOWARDS IDENTITY

NO 13
The Dead Lake by Hamid Ismailov
Translated from the Russian by Andrew Bromfield
'Immense poetic power.' GUARDIAN

NO 14
The Blue Room by Hanne Ørstavik
Translated from the Norwegian by Deborah Dawkin
'Shrewd and psychologically adroit.' LANCASHIRE
EVENING POST

NO 15
Under the Tripoli Sky by Kamal Ben Hameda
Translated from the French by Adriana Hunter
'Beautifully simple and restrained prose.'
HUFFINGTON POST

....
NEW IN 2015 . CHANCE ENCOUNTER: MEETING THE OTHER

NO 16
White Hunger by Aki Ollikainen
Translated from the Finnish by Emily Jeremiah and Fleur Jeremiah
'A novella that feels like a huge, great novel.'
SATAKUNNAN KANSA

NO 17
Reader For Hire by Raymond Jean
Translated from the French by Adriana Hunter
'A book that will make you want to read more books.'
COSMOPOLITAN

NO 18
The Looking-Glass Sisters by Gøhril Gabrielsen
Translated from the Norwegian by John Irons
*'Raw and dark and wonderfully different from
anything else.'* DAG OG TID

Peirene Press is proud to support the Maya Centre.

The Maya Centre

counselling for women

The Maya Centre provides free psychodynamic counselling and group psychotherapy for women on low incomes in London. The counselling is offered in many different languages, including Arabic, Turkish and Portuguese. The centre also undertakes educational work on women's mental health issues.

By buying this book you help the Maya Centre to continue their pioneering services.
Peirene Press will donate 50p from the sale of this book to the Maya Centre.

www.mayacentre.org.uk